Alyosha's Apple

Alyosha's Apple

A Tale
of Old Russia

told by Alvin Alexsi Currier
& Illustrated by Nadja Glazunova

Conciliar Press

BEN LOMOND, CALIFORNIA

Published by Conciliar Press, P.O. Box 76, Ben Lomond, California
Printed in Hong Kong

Photo of Nadja Glazunova (page 23) by Pat Eggert, County News, Menomonie, Wisconsin.
Photo of Alvin Alexsi Currier (page 24) by Kirsti Jantunen, Helsinki, Finland.

Library of Congress Cataloging-in-Publication Data

Currier, Alvin Alexsi.
    Alyosha's apple : a tale of Old Russia / told by Alvin Alexsi Currier ; illustrated by Nadja Glazunova.
           p.   cm.
    Summary: After an orphaned girl in Old Russia walks deep into the forest to visit a hermit who prays
for her brother's healing, she returns home to a wonderful sight.
        ISBN 1-888212-08-X
        [1. Miracles—Fiction.   2. Brothers and sisters—Fiction.   3. Orphans—Fiction.
        4. Folklore—Russia.   5. Stories in rhyme.]
    I. Glazunova, Nadja, ill.   II. Title.
    PZ8.3.C933A1 1997
    [E]—dc21   97-3741
                                                                         CIP
                                                                         AC

L ong, long ago,
    in a very small cottage
    in a far distant village,
deep, deep in the woods,
way in the north of old Russia,
a mother lay dying.
Nearing her death,
to her daughter she whispered
with her very last breath,
"Pray, my child, pray,
pray in all that you do,
pray, my darling,
and God will bless you."
Then her hand raised in blessing,
fell limp on the bed,
and the child knew
that her mother was dead.

So starts the story of Tanya, the orphan,
who cared for her brother, Alyosha by name,
who stayed in his bed, for, alas, he was lame.
So starts the story of two orphans' prayers,
for morning, noon, and night they prayed.
They prayed for their mother, who was with them no more.
They prayed for their father, who was killed in the war.
They prayed in the spring, when the seed was sowed.
They prayed in the summer, when the hay was mowed.
They prayed in the fall, when the harvest came in.
They prayed in the winter, with its snow and wind.
With Tanya kneeling, Alyosha in bed,
together their prayers were faithfully said.
Only one prayer prayed Tanya alone:
From morning's light when the church bells pealed
to evening's dark when the door was sealed,
continually Tanya silently cried,
"Please, Mother of God, let my brother be healed."

So it came to pass on one cool night,
quite near the end of summer,
when her prayers were said
Tanya made her bed
on the warmth of the big stone oven.
As the darkness grew deep,
she fell fast asleep,
but before too long she sensed a song.
She heard a bird,
so it seemed in her dream,
and then from the bird, an angel appeared,
and out of the song words were heard.
The angel said, "Have no fear!
I bring you a message, so listen and hear.
When you awake by the dawn's dim light,
slip out of the village in the fading night.
Follow the path to the forest; run!
Hurry along in the rising sun,
and there as a bird I will come to meet you,
there as a bird I will wait to greet you.
All I can tell you is your prayers have been heard.
Remember, remember, follow the bird."

It still seemed that she dreamed
as the night turned gray
with the dawning of day,
and she slipped away
through the mists and the fog to the forest.
Suddenly there, she awoke to fear.
Wild beasts were near.
The darkness around
was filled with sounds
and she grew weak with terror.
"Holy Mother of God," she gasped in prayer,
and as she did, she suddenly heard
the sweetest sound of a tiny bird,
and in a flash, she saw a splash
of winging, singing color.
As she saw the bird and its song she heard,
her heart burst with joy and thanksgiving.
Fearlessly now she followed along,
fearlessly now she followed the song,
over the ridges and through the glades,
across the creeks in the shifting shade,
into the day she made her way
ever deeper into the forest.

They had come a long way,
it was nearly midday,
when Tanya felt in the air
something awesome and rare
in the shade of the glade before her.
She did not fear,
yet she sensed she was near
to something that must be most wondrous.
So cautiously she rounded a tree,
and did suddenly see
the cause of the spell she'd been feeling.
Before her sat a holy man,
a hermit monk of the forest,
an elder at peace and hallowed by prayer—
and before him stood a big brown bear!
He turned, he smiled, and he waved her near,
then softly he asked, "Tell me why you've come here."
"I've come for my brother," she quickly replied.
"For he cannot stand, or rise from his bed.
Yet his heart is so warm, his spirit so bright,
he has even learned to read and write,
but as I have said,
he can never, ever get out of bed."
Mercy filled the old man's eyes,
then crossing himself he slowly stood up
and beckoned Tanya into his hut.

Tanya followed the monk into his cell,
but what happened next, she never could tell.
She clearly remembered he knelt in prayer,
so she knelt down behind him there.
But as his prayers flowed on longer,
echoes entered ever stronger.
Echoes? No! Others praying,
angels, saints, around him swaying,
God's great kingdom gathered down,
hosts of heaven circling round,
choruses of swirling sound,
waves of prayers, heaven bound.
Next a scent of incense swelled,
a heavenly sweetness soon they smelled,
and when Alyosha's name was prayed,
in the cell appeared a light.
The elder, the icons, were shining bright,
dazzling, blinding, beyond all sight.

At that very moment, miles away,
in the tiny village of Tanya's home,
in the cottage she shared with her brother,
the scent of incense began to seep,
and Alyosha, alert, sat up in his bed.
Then he sensed a sound
with the sweetness he smelled.
Somewhere near, he could hear—
he knew not from where—
a choir was singing,
was chanting a prayer.
Scent and singing quickly swelled,
all around him ringing.
Then suddenly clear one voice drew near,
and beside his bed a light grew bright,
and his blinking eyes beheld the sight
of a holy elder before him.
No words were said as he stood by the bed,
but his eyes were filled with mercy.
One hand reached out to Alyosha's head,
the other hand held something red.
The monk was offering an apple.
Shyly Alyosha accepted the treat,
but as he began the fruit to eat,
he sensed a tingling in his feet,
then all along his legs' whole length,
he felt a growing, rising strength.

B ack in the forest, at the end of the prayer,
Tanya knew it was time to head home from there.
She thanked the monk with all her heart
and asked his blessing to depart,
but as she turned to the forest trail
she was seized with fear and turned quite pale.
"Please, Mother of God," she whispered in prayer,
"Please, oh please, keep me safe in there."
And just then the monk said he had been thinking
his bear should go too, to protect her.
Oh! What a sight, in the afternoon light,
bird, child, and bear in the forest.
Running and walking, singing and talking,
they wound their way in the fading day,
until far away they heard the bells,
calling the village for evening prayer.
Touchingly Tanya told Misha the bear
that he must not dare
give his scent to the dogs of the village,
so she said "Good-bye," and heaved a sigh,
and patted him gently in parting.
Crossing herself, she turned away,
and quickly now she ran down the ridge,
crossed over the bridge,
and cut through the fields toward the village.

The church bells were singing
as Tanya passed, running fast,
down the lane of her village.
Clucking chickens scattering flew.
As she rounded a corner, there came into view
the doorway of her cottage.
Then her eyes grew wide in amazement.
Alyosha, her brother, was standing there,
in answer to prayer,
no longer in bed, but standing instead.
As his sister he spied, "Tanya!" he cried,
and together they flew,
tumbling out their stories.
"The hermit's cell—I was there,
with the elder in prayer."
"But he was here, I saw him so clear,
and he gave me the apple of healing."
Then gasping for air,
they both came aware
that the bells had stopped their ringing.
At once they knew what they had to do,
so hand in hand they ran to stand
in the church, to join in the singing.
In joy and awe, they gave thanks to God
for the miracle of His mercy.

About the Illustrator

Nadja Glazunova began her artistic career in a Soviet factory, painting floral patterns on wooden souvenirs. Her obvious talent won her admission to the National College of Traditional and Folk Art, where she studied the work of such masters as Ivan Bilibin, and met her husband, Leonid, a master woodcarver. After graduation, they made their home in Petrozavodsk, near the Finnish border, and supported themselves by selling their joint artwork—Nadja painting what Leonid carved.

In 1988 the Glazunovs met Alvin Currier, who immediately recognized Nadja's talent and determined to bring her work to a wider audience. Nadja painted a series of scenes from old Russian life which have been produced as prints and notecards and distributed internationally. She also collaborated with Currier on a previous book, *The Miraculous Child.*

Nadja's work, full of color, life, and joy, brings the spirit of Orthodox Russia to life. Her dream is to see her beloved country return to the kind of life, based on the faith and traditions of Orthodoxy, that she depicts in her paintings. She uses the proceeds of her work to help less fortunate friends and to contribute to the restoration of churches which were neglected or destroyed under communism. The Glazunovs now live in the monastery city of Sergiev-Posad.

About the Author

Outwardly Alvin Alexsi Currier is known as a son of the city of Minneapolis, and until retirement after 35 years, he was classified professionally as a Presbyterian minister who served various midwestern American churches, two parishes in Germany, and for eleven years as a college chaplain.

Inwardly he is a pilgrim, who sensing his spiritual emptiness, fled professional life for the forest in 1975. There in the following two decades he lived as a monastic, created St. Herman's Hermitage, and found his spiritual home in the Orthodox Church.

Today with his wife Anastasia he lives in St. Paul, Minnesota, as an author, artist, and interpreter of Orthodoxy, traveling widely in Eastern Europe and organizing tours for others to experience Orthodoxy from the inside out. His previous books include *Karelia : An Introduction to and Meditation on Karelian Orthodox Culture* and *The Miraculous Child.*